Acorn whinnied softly as if to say, "I don't understand. Why are you crying?"

"Oh, Acorn," Anna sobbed, "I don't want to lose you. And I don't want you to lose me."

PONY PALS
A Pony For Keeps

Jeanne Betancourt
Illustrations By Charlotte Alder

For Anika Marissa Murray

The author thanks Elvia Gignoux for generously sharing her lifelong knowledge and love of horses.

Thanks also to Shirley Kokesh and the fifth-grade girls at Kildonan Elementary School, particularly Hannah Charlap

Scholastic Children's Books,
Euston House, 24 Eversholt Street
London NW1 1DB, UK
A division of Scholastic Ltd
London ~ New York ~ Toronto ~ Sydney ~ Auckland
Mexico City ~ New Delhi ~ Hong Kong

First published in the US by Scholastic Inc., 1995
This edition published in the UK by Scholastic Ltd, 2006

10 digit ISBN 0 439 95131 3
13 digit ISBN 978 0 439 95131 9

Printed and bound by Nørhaven Paperback A/S, Denmark

1 2 3 4 5 6 7 8 9 10

The right of Jeanne Betancourt and Charlotte Alder to be identified as the author
and illustrator of this work respectively has been asserted by them in accordance with
the Copyright, Designs and Patents Act, 1988.

Papers used by Scholastic Children's Books are made from wood grown
in sustainable forests.

Contents

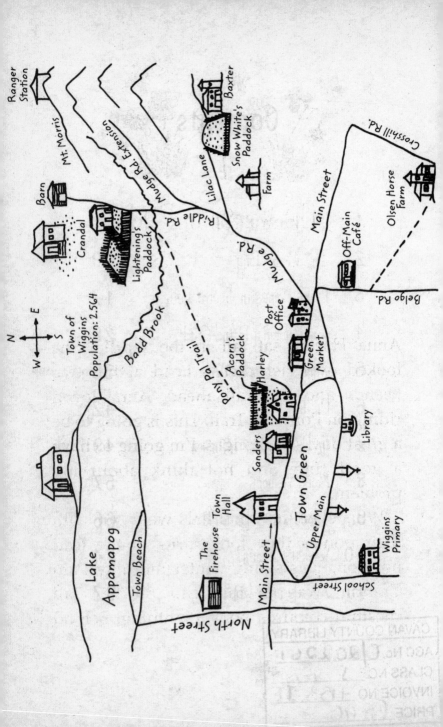

1

The Woman in Red

Anna Harley sat tall in the saddle. She looked over her pony's head at her two friends and the trail ahead. Anna loved riding on Pony Pal Trail. This is going to be a great day, she thought. I'm going to have a good time and not think about my problem.

Whenever the Pony Pals went out with their ponies they took turns in the lead position. This sunny winter morning Pam Crandal was in the lead on her tall chestnut-coloured pony, Lightning. Behind

1

her was Lulu Sanders on Snow White. Then came Anna on her little brown and black Shetland pony, Acorn.

The Pony Pals reached a long, straight stretch of trail. Pam moved Lightning into a trot and then a canter. Lulu and Snow White picked up their pace. Anna squeezed her legs against Acorn's side. "Come on, Acorn," she said. "Faster."

But Acorn slowed down instead.

Anna patiently waited for him to decide whether to keep up with the others.

Suddenly Acorn snorted and charged ahead so fast that Anna thought they might climb right up Snow White's back. "Whoa," Anna called out as she shifted her position in the saddle and pulled on the reins. But, as usual, Acorn stopped when he decided that it was time to stop.

Lulu turned Snow White around to face Anna and Acorn. "Is Acorn being the boss again today?" Lulu asked.

Anna felt a little embarrassed that she couldn't always control her pony. But she

joked, "So what else is new?"

Pam turned Lightning around to face the other Pony Pals. "Let's go onto the Wiggins estate," she said excitedly. She pointed to a space between the trees. "We can get on a trail over there." Lightning pawed the ground and whinnied as if to agree.

"But look," Lulu said, "there's some new *No Trespassing* signs."

"They're for hunters," Pam said. "Not for kids on their ponies."

"The riding trails are great in there," Lulu added. "We had fun the last time we went."

Anna looked from Pam to Lulu. "You guys just want to jump your ponies," she said.

"These are the best conditions we've had this winter for jumping," Pam said. "No snow. No ice. No mud."

Lulu leaned over and stroked Snow White's smooth white neck. "Snow White loves to jump."

"Come on, Anna," Pam said. "Maybe

today's the day Acorn will finally jump for you."

Lulu reached over and scratched Acorn's neck through his black mane. "We all know you can do it, Acorn," she said.

"OK," Anna finally agreed. "Let's go."

Even though Acorn wouldn't jump, Anna had fun on the trails. Her little pony was surefooted and smart. He loved the challenge of finding ways around the fallen logs that Lightning and Snow White jumped over. I could go almost anywhere on my pony, Anna thought. He's clever and brave. Who cares if he won't jump for me?

The Pony Pals went further into the Wiggins estate than they'd ever gone before. After a while they got off their ponies and let them drink from Badd Brook. Through the leafless trees the girls could see Wiggins mansion in the distance.

"That Wiggins lady must be so weird to live in a big place like that all by herself," Anna said. "I heard it has twenty-seven

rooms, not counting the bathrooms."

"I bet she hasn't left there in twenty-seven years," Lulu said.

"And has at least twenty-seven cats," Pam added.

"And hasn't taken a bath in twenty-seven weeks," Anna kidded. "Or brushed her teeth."

"Gross!" they all screamed. The Pony Pals giggled.

Suddenly Anna stopped laughing. "I wonder what she would do if she found us here?"

"Probably take us prisoners," Pam teased. "Like Hansel and Gretel."

Lulu cackled like a witch. "I'll eat you up, my pretties."

"You guys," Anna whispered. "Someone's riding a horse out of the barn. Look."

Anna pointed to a distant shape. She could make out that it was a rider dressed in red on a big black horse.

"I bet it's her," Lulu said.

6

"And she's coming this way," Pam added. "Let's get out of here."

The girls quickly mounted their ponies and galloped towards Pony Pal Trail.

Even though he was the smallest, Acorn kept up with Snow White and Lightning. As they galloped along Anna thought, Acorn, you always come through for me when it's really important.

When the girls reached Pony Pal Trail, Anna and Lulu said goodbye to Pam. The woodland trail connected Acorn's and Snow White's paddock with Lightning's paddock.

Pam and Lightning headed toward her house at the north end of Pony Pal Trail. Anna and Lulu waved and then walked their ponies along. "Tonight I'll write to Rema Baxter and tell her that we practised jumping," Lulu said.

Anna remembered how the Pony Pals helped Snow White recover from her terrible accident. And then how they worked together to convince Rema Baxter and her

parents to let Lulu take care of Snow White.

"You shouldn't have to keep writing all that stuff down," Anna said. "It's like Rema's giving you homework. She should just be thankful you saved Snow White's life."

"She is," Lulu said. "That's why she's letting me take care of Snow White until she gets back from boarding school."

"How could Rema leave Snow White just for a chance to go to a different school?" Anna asked.

"Maybe it's a really good school and she likes to study or something," Lulu said.

Anna couldn't imagine giving up Acorn for schoolwork. Then she remembered the problem she'd managed to forget about all morning. Tears sprung to her eyes as the awful truth came back to her. She was going to have to give up her pony because of school, too. Only in her case the problem was because she hated school, not because she loved it.

2

The Wrong Pony

Back at their ponies' shelter, Anna and Lulu removed saddles and bridles. Then they led the ponies out into the paddock they shared behind Anna's house. Anna watched Snow White run after Acorn to a far corner of the field.

Anna loved that the ponies got along so well. Just like the Pony Pals, she thought.

Anna and Pam had been best friends since kindergarten. Pam liked to be in charge and was very clever. She always did well in school. Pam knew lots about

animals, too, especially horses. She'd been around them all her life because her dad was a large-animal veterinarian and her mother was a riding instructor.

Anna thought about her other best friend, Lulu. Lulu and her dad lived in England for two years. That's where Lulu learned all about ponies and how to ride them. Now Lulu was staying with her grandmother in the house next door. Lulu's father was studying wildlife in the Amazon jungle while Lulu was living in Wiggins. Anna knew that Lulu missed her father a lot. She was really close to her dad, especially because her mother died when she was four. Lulu wasn't sad though; she was a happy, adventurous person. She loved exploring nature like her father and had great ideas about things to do outdoors.

Anna thought about her own parents. Her father built houses, so he got to work outdoors. Her mother worked indoors because she owned a café and catered parties. Anna was the person in her family

who loved animals the most. She especially liked ponies.

In the paddock Snow White and Acorn were nose to nose, sniffing, nibbling, and nickering at one another. Anna thought, the Pony Pals are three best friends with three wonderful ponies. Now I'm going to spoil it.

"Look at Acorn and Snow White," Lulu said. "It's sad to think that they'll be separated when Rema comes home."

"They're going to be separated sooner than that," Anna mumbled.

"Why?" Lulu asked. "Did your parents say Snow White can't stay here?"

"Snow White can stay," Anna said. "It's Acorn who has to leave."

Lulu was shocked. "Why does Acorn have to leave?" she asked.

"Because I don't do well in school like you and Pam," Anna explained. "My parents said they won't let me buy Acorn unless my marks go up. When report cards come out I'll have to give him back to the

man we leased him from."

"You can get better marks, Anna," Lulu said. "You're really clever. You get low marks because you don't like to write. Listen – Pam and I will help you get ready for the unit tests next week."

Anna didn't tell Lulu that no matter how much she studied, she still couldn't get passing marks on tests. She had no trouble understanding what went on in class but she couldn't do the written work. And she could hardly read a sentence without coming across words she didn't know.

Their Year Five teacher, Mr Livingston, gave her extra homework in reading and maths. But it wasn't working. She still made the same stupid mistakes. Sometimes she got so fed up that she just doodled and made pictures of ponies.

"Why didn't you tell me about this before?" Lulu asked. "Pam and I could have been helping you all this time."

"I don't know," Anna said. "I just didn't."

That night as Anna said good night to Acorn, she thought about why she didn't tell Lulu and Pam. She knew it was because she felt ashamed that she couldn't read or write like her friends. "Oh, Acorn," Anna said, "maybe, just maybe, the Pony Pals can help me." Anna stroked Acorn's neck. "If I study out loud with them maybe I'll get better marks on that stupid report card." She gave Acorn a big hug good night. "Then I can keep you."

Sunday morning, after chores, Anna and Lulu saddled up their ponies and rode over to Pam's place on Pony Pal Trail. Pam's five-year-old twin brother and sister, Jack and Jill, were waiting for them.

"Can I ride Acorn?" they shouted together.

Anna laughed and told Mrs Crandal she didn't mind if the twins rode her pony. "Thanks so much," Mrs Crandal said. "I'd love to give them a chance to ride."

"It'll be fun for Acorn, too," said Anna.

Mrs Crandal went to the barn to get two

riding helmets. A few minutes later, the Pony Pals watched her and the twins go onto the trail with Acorn.

"Would you ride Snow White?" Lulu asked Anna. "Rema said other people should ride her so she doesn't become too attached to me."

"Rema Baxter's nutty," Anna said. "But I'll do it for you."

Even though Snow White was quite a bit higher than Acorn, Anna swung easily into the saddle. She adjusted the stirrups to her own height and then rode around the outside of the field. Anna was amazed at how responsive Snow White was to her commands. It took only the slightest shift in her weight and a squeeze of her legs to move from a walk to a trot to a canter.

Then, almost without thinking, Anna turned Snow White to the centre of the field. They faced three low jumps that Mrs Crandal had set up. Anna directed Snow White over them. Jumping felt wonderful. Anna felt as if she and Snow White were

floating. Anna remembered how much she loved jumping in riding school.

As she slowed Snow White down to a walk, Anna looked anxiously toward Pony Pal Trail. She was relieved that Acorn hadn't seen her riding and jumping on another pony. She didn't want his feelings to be hurt.

Lulu and Pam clapped for Anna and Snow White.

"I forgot what a terrific jumper you are, Anna," Pam said. "You have great timing and balance."

"Wow," Lulu said. "I didn't even know you could jump. Why won't Acorn do jumps?"

"I don't know," Anna said.

"Maybe Acorn's just the wrong pony for you, Anna," Pam suggested.

Anna answered angrily, "Acorn is the right pony for me." She dismounted Snow White and handed the reins to Lulu. "Jumping is no big deal."

3

Eight Homes in Twelve Years

"I've schooled a lot of ponies," Mrs Crandal said. "But I've never met one quite as stubborn as your Acorn." The Pony Pals were sitting in the Crandals' kitchen eating lunch.

Anna felt angry at everyone – including Mrs Crandal – for criticizing Acorn. She felt a little better when Mrs Crandal added, "And I've never met a pony quite as bright. I wonder who owned him before and how he was treated. Did you lease him from Reggie Olson?"

Anna nodded.

"Who's Reggie Olson?" Lulu asked.

"Reggie Olson has a big horse farm over on Crosshill Road," Pam explained. "A lot of people with horses around here get them from him."

"What's his farm like?" Lulu asked.

"Oh it's a really cool place," Anna answered. She was remembering the happy day when she looked at five pretty ponies in a field and picked out Acorn – the cutest one of all.

"You know," Mrs Crandal said. "I haven't been over to Olson's place in ages. And we'll be getting the twins their first ponies soon. It'd be fun to check out his stock."

"And we could find out more about Acorn," Pam said.

Mrs Crandal and the three girls made a plan. The next day she and the twins would pick them up after school and go together over to the Olson farm. But that was tomorrow. Right now the Pony Pals had some studying to do. They went up to Pam's room and took out their school books.

"Just stick with us," Lulu told Anna, "and you'll ace the tests."

Anna tried very hard to believe Lulu. And she tried very hard to study with her friends.

First they quizzed one another on science vocabulary. Anna learned the meanings easily when they drilled them out loud. But she was too embarrassed to tell her friends that she couldn't read some of words.

"Let's review maths," Lulu suggested.

When Pam read a word problem out loud, Anna knew how to get the answer. But she couldn't remember the multiplication tables she needed to finish the problem.

Later, as Anna and Lulu mounted their ponies to ride home, Pam said, "Anna, you should write the times tables out five times each tonight."

"Maybe you should say them out loud as you write," Lulu added.

Anna didn't tell them that the week

before she'd written out all the times tables ten times each.

The next afternoon, the Pony Pals were rushing to get their jackets from their lockers. They were excited to go to Olson's farm.

"How'd you do on the maths test?" Lulu asked Anna.

"OK," Anna said, even though she worked so slowly she'd only finished half the test.

Pam patted her on the back. "That's great. I just know you'll be able to keep Acorn."

The Olson farm was even bigger than Anna remembered. There were three paddocks with horses and ponies. And a yellow barn with clean, brightly lit horse stalls.

"I guess the last time I was here I only paid attention to Acorn," Anna said. "I don't remember seeing all those horses."

Mr Olson, a white-haired man in jeans

and a plaid jacket, gave them a tour of the paddocks and barns.

The twins were picking out the ponies they wanted. Sometimes the same one. "I saw that red one first so its mine," Jill shouted excitedly.

"It's already mine," Jack said. "I saw it first. I just didn't tell you."

Mrs Crandal reminded her children that they weren't getting ponies that day. "Or ever," she scolded, "if you two don't stop arguing."

Mr Olson walked over to the Pony Pals. He smiled at Anna. "How's Acorn doing?" he asked.

"OK," Anna answered.

"We were wondering why Acorn's so bossy," Lulu said.

"He's not bossy," Anna said. "He just has a mind of his own."

"Maybe you want to be riding a horse instead of a pony," Mr Olson said. He pointed to a handsome black horse looking over the paddock fence. "That Morgan is a

honey. Shouldn't be too big for you. I'd be happy to get Acorn back. I have another family looking to buy a pony just like him."

"I'm not too big for Acorn," Anna said. "And I won't be for a long time. Maybe never. Everyone in my family is short."

"Does that mean you'll be wanting to buy him then?" Mr Olson asked.

"Yes," Anna answered. Her heart was pounding in her chest. I have to keep Acorn, she thought, I just have to.

"Well then," Mr Olson said, "I might as well go over to the office and print out the terms of the sale. You can take the papers home with you. Save me the stamp." He turned and walked away.

Pam signalled to Lulu and Anna that they should go with Mr Olson. Mr Olson seemed surprised that the girls were walking alongside him toward the office.

Anna had an idea why Acorn was so strong-willed. "Has Acorn had a lot of different people leasing him?" she asked Mr Olson.

"As ponies go," he said thoughtfully, "I'd have to say Acorn's had quite a few homes."

"Didn't anyone ever want to buy him before?" Lulu asked.

"One family bought him a couple of years ago. But they moved to a big city and couldn't keep him. So I bought him back." With that, Mr Olson opened the door to his office. The girls came in behind him.

He went over to his computer. "This will only take a minute," he said. The three girls watched him type T-E-R-M-S O-F S-A-L-E on the computer keyboard.

"Do you have a list of all the people Acorn's lived with?" Anna asked.

"Sure I do," he answered.

"I just love computers," Pam said. She winked at Lulu and Anna. "Could you show us how you keep the names of all the people who've leased or owned Acorn?"

Mr Olson liked showing off his computer programme almost as much as he liked showing off his ponies and horses. The

three girls hovered over his shoulder and watched the screen as he typed A-C-O-R-N. In a split second, a list of eight names and addresses appeared on the screen.

Even Mr Olson was surprised at how many names were listed. "Eight homes in twelve years," he said. "That's a lot of different places for one pony to live. But that Shetland is tough."

Anna wondered what it was like for Acorn to have lived in so many different homes and to have had so many owners. They must have all treated him differently. And just when he got used to one family, he'd be moved to another. She saw that her own name and address were at the end of the list. Whose name would come next?

Mr Olson typed again and said, "Miss Harley, do you want to buy the saddle and bridle with the pony?"

"Yes," Anna answered.

A few minutes later Mr Olson printed out two copies of then terms of the sale. He put them in an envelope and handed it to

Anna. "If your parents have any questions have them give me a call," he told her. "As soon as they give me back a signed copy with a cheque, Acorn is yours."

Anna took the papers. I've got to get good marks on my report card, she thought. I have to keep Acorn.

When the Pony Pals were outside they tried to remember the list of people who had leased or owned Acorn. All Anna could remember was how sad the long list made her feel.

"I noticed that only two of the people he lived with were from Wiggins," Pam said.

"Didn't you guys see?" Lulu asked excitedly. "Tommy Rand was on that list!"

"Tommy Rand?" Anna asked. "Are you sure?"

"I'm sure," Lulu said. "He leased Acorn four years ago."

"Poor Acorn!" Anna exclaimed.

The girls talked about Tommy Rand all the way home from Olson's farm.

"He's the meanest kid in Year Eight," Pam said.

"The bossiest, too," Lulu added. "I hate how he orders us around when he's break monitor."

"Acorn hates bossy people," Anna said.

"Maybe he was nicer when he was younger," Lulu suggested.

"Or nicer to animals than people," Pam added. "I meet lots of people at our animal clinic who are like that."

"I doubt it," Anna said. "But I have to find out for sure."

4

What Tommy Rand Said

The next day, as the three Pony Pals slowly moved along the school canteen line, Lulu whispered into Anna's ear, "There he is."

Anna looked up to see the tall, mean-looking Tommy Rand walking across the canteen with a lunch tray. She was scared, but she was determined to find out how Tommy Rand treated Acorn.

Anna reached Tommy Rand as he sat down at a table with the other Year Eight boys.

"Hi," she said. She held up her notebook.

"I'm Anna Harley and I'm doing a report on kids and their animals. I would like to interview you."

"Why me?" Tommy Rand said. "Ask someone your own age."

Anna persisted. "I know you had a Shetland pony when you were in Year Four. I was wondering if you could tell me what the pony was like."

"That was just a kid thing," he said. "I don't even remember its name."

Anna was so shocked at this that she blurted out, "Don't you miss him?"

She realized that Lulu and Pam were now standing next to her. Her friends made her feel more confident. "His name is Acorn," she told Tommy Rand.

"Did he ever jump for you?" Lulu asked.

"Why did you send him back to Mr Olson?" Pam asked. "Why didn't you keep Acorn? Were you too lazy to take care of him?"

"Get lost," Tommy Rand said.

The Year Eight boys were laughing so

hard that a teacher had to come over to quiet them down. But by then the Pony Pals were boldly marching to the Year Five table on the other side of the room.

Anna didn't care that everyone was staring at them. All she cared about was that she had to pass her science test that afternoon. No matter what, she had to protect Acorn from ever, ever having to be around another kid like Tommy Rand.

Even while they ate, Pam and Lulu helped Anna review the science lesson on the parts of the flower.

After dinner that night Anna told her mother, "I'm going out to check on the ponies."

"You better get to your homework," her father said.

Anna held up a folder and a flashlight. "I'll study out there," she said.

"Don't you think you'll be able to concentrate better in you room, at your desk?" her father asked.

"Just remember," her mother warned. "If your marks haven't gone up, no more pony."

Anna's older sister Tammy looked up from her magazine. "Can't you guys just leave her alone? Maybe she's doing the best she can."

"I doubt it," their father said. He put his arm around Anna and gave her a hug. "I know this girl. Her brain is as good as yours and her brother's. All my kids are bright. Anna's too easily distracted and draws when she should be writing. Seems to me that Acorn is the biggest distraction of all."

Anna wiggled away from her father's hug and went toward the back door. "Be right back," she said. She bolted out of the house full of anger and sadness.

Anna felt better after she ran through the yard and climbed the fence into the paddock. It was a beautiful night. The stars were sparkling in the dark sky.

It wasn't too cold for Anna in the shelter.

31

Not with two warm ponies nearby. She sat on an empty feed bucket. Acorn came right over and nuzzled against her shoulder. .

"How you doing, sweet pony?" she asked.

Acorn whinnied happily.

"You're right," she said. "I do have a treat for you." She reached in her pocket and gave Acorn an apple. Snow White, who'd been sleeping standing up on the other side of the shelter, woke up and came trotting over to her.

Anna laughed. "You were sleeping," she told the white pony. "How did you know I had an apple for you?" Snow White ate her apple. When she was sure there weren't any more treats, Snow White went back to her corner of the shelter. Soon she dropped her head and fell back to sleep.

But Acorn stayed wide-awake and as close to Anna as he could get. "Acorn, I do terribly in school. Sometimes I can get a good mark by doing oral reports or artwork instead of essays. But even with

Pam and Lulu helping me I don't pass my tests. I can't read well. I know I'm mixing up some of my letters and words. And it's getting harder and harder to fool people about that. Sometimes I can't even read the questions on a test."

Acorn whinnied softly as if to say, "I don't understand. Why are you crying?"

"Oh, Acorn," she sobbed, "I don't want to lose you. And I don't want you to lose me." She put her arms around his neck and hugged him. "I don't care if you never, ever jump. I don't care that you decide when to go and when to stop. I don't even care anymore why you behave the way you do. I just don't want to lose you. And I don't want you to have to go live with another mean kid like Tommy Rand."

She wiped her tears and opened the folder with the lists of spelling words. Acorn stayed right beside her as she copied the letters of the spelling words over and over.

5

Anna's Report card

Monday, five minutes before the end of the school day, Mr Livingston stood at the front of the room with a pile of envelopes in his hands. "Come up for your report cards when I call your name," he directed. "We'll go alphabetically by last name."

Anna's heart was pounding in her throat. She was praying, Please, please let my marks go up.

"Crandal, Pam," was the first Pony Pal to receive her report card. Anna knew that Pam would get all A's. Like always. And

that her parents would take her out to dinner to celebrate. Like always.

Three names later Mr Livingston called out, "Harley, Anna." As Anna walked to the front of the room she thought she could see that Mr Livingston was disappointed in her.

She managed to whisper, "Thank you," as he placed the envelope in her opened hand.

Walking back to her desk she could feel that there was more than the thin report card in the envelope. She knew from past experience what a thick report card envelope meant. It was a sure sign she had failed. Inside her report card there would be a letter to her parents. The letter would ask them to set up a meeting with Mr Livingston.

A few minutes later school was out. The Pony Pals headed towards Main Street together.

When they were out of earshot of other kids, Lulu said, "Anna, you have to open it sometime."

Pam tried to sound optimistic. "Maybe

the letter is to your mother asking her to cater something."

"Yeah," Lulu agreed. "Or to your dad about doing a building job for Mr Livingston. It doesn't have to be about you."

Anna didn't say anything.

Finally, when they were in Lulu's grandmother's kitchen getting a snack, Anna let Lulu open the envelope and look at her report card.

"You were right," Lulu told Anna sadly.

Pam looked over Lulu's shoulder to see Anna's marks. "We've got to talk to your parents ourselves. We can't let them take Acorn away from you."

"We didn't have enough time to help you," Lulu complained. "We'll tell your mother that from now on we'll study together every—"

Anna interrupted her. "Don't you understand? It won't make any difference." She took the report card from Lulu and finally looked at it. She got a C in social studies,

C– in science, D in maths, and D in English. The same marks as last time. "I didn't improve in one subject," she said sadly. "And my parents said if I didn't get better marks I couldn't keep Acorn. They never, ever go back on their word."

"But look, you got an A in art," Pam told Anna. "And Mr Livingston wrote 'Lively participant in class discussions, eager to learn' next to your social studies mark."

"And you had perfect attendance," Lulu said. "Those things should count for something."

That evening, Anna waited until her brother and sister had left for a school basketball game before showing her parents her report card. Anna was nervous when they sat around the kitchen table to talk about her marks.

"Well, it's settled," her father said. "The pony goes back to Reggie Olson."

Anna had promised herself she wouldn't cry. But still she burst into tears.

"Now, now, Anna," her mother said, "maybe in a couple of years you can get another pony. Or a horse."

"It's partly our fault," her father said. "We thought having the pony would motivate you to work harder at school. But I can see now it's been too much."

Her mother reached over and took her hand. "Anna, sweetie, please stop crying. That won't help. I bet Pam and Lulu will be very generous about letting you ride their ponies. After all, Snow White is right in your own backyard."

"I'm not crying for myself," Anna said. "I'm crying for Acorn."

"But why?" her mother asked. "I'm sure another family will take very good care of Acorn."

"Besides," her father said with a little smile, "that pony knows how to take care of himself."

Her mother added, "Remember, we're only doing this for your own good."

"Nobody understands," Anna sobbed.

"It's awful for Acorn and it's awful for me." She shoved her chair back from the table, jumped up, and ran out the back door to find her pony.

That night Anna dreamt that she went to Mr Olson's farm to see Acorn. Mr Olson told her that he had sold Acorn to Tommy Rand. He handed her a piece of paper with Tommy Rand's address. But Anna couldn't read the address. All the letters on the paper and on the street signs looked jumbled to her. She ran all over Wiggins looking for help. But no one could help her. Anna woke up in the middle of the night crying and out of breath.

6
On the Run

The next morning, as Anna and Lulu were putting out fresh hay for their ponies, Anna pretended to cough four times. "I have a cold," she told Lulu. "My mother said I should stay home from school today."

"Don't worry," Lulu said. "Pam and I will come visit you after school. We've got to work out a way for you to keep Acorn."

"It's no use," Anna told her. "My parents aren't going to change their minds."

Back in the house, Anna packed up her book bag and acted as if she were going to

42

school. When she opened the front door to leave, she heard her father say to her mother, "I think Anna's accepted that the pony has to go."

Instead of walking to school, Anna sneaked into her backyard and hid in the bushes along the edge of the paddock. Acorn came galloping over to greet her. She whispered to her pony, "I'm going to spend all day with you."

Anna watched her house. First, she saw her brother and sister get on the school bus that would take them to Eleanor Roosevelt Regional High. Next, her father backed out of the driveway in his red pickup truck. Finally, Anna saw her mother walk down Main Street toward her café. Now that she was sure her family was gone, Anna sneaked back into the house and packed up some water and food. She left plenty of room in her saddlebag for Acorn's favourite oats.

Back in the paddock she prepared Acorn for a ride. While she worked, Snow White stood by watching. When Anna led Acorn

43

to the gate at the beginning of Pony Pal Trail, Snow White walked along beside them. Finally, Anna and Acorn were on the trail side of the gate. Snow White remained on the paddock side. Anna mounted Acorn and said, "Let's go."

Acorn stood still.

"What's wrong?" Anna asked. "You like to go on Pony Pal Trail."

Snow White whinnied. Acorn whinnied back. And Anna realized that Acorn didn't want to leave his friend. She felt sad. How many times had Acorn been separated from people and animals that he'd been attached to? He'd had eight different homes in twelve years. Now it would be nine. And it was her fault.

Anna looked behind them to be sure Snow White was all right. The pony was gaily galloping around the paddock.

"Come on, Acorn," Anna said. "We're going for a ride."

Acorn didn't move.

Anna squeezed her legs against his sides.

"Please, Acorn," she said, "don't do this to me now." But Acorn still didn't move.

Anna remembered what Mrs Crandal told her about riding a pony who'd developed bad habits. "You're the one in charge," she'd said. "If you let Acorn know that, he will work with you. Then you can think through him and the two of you will move as one. But if the pony's in charge, you can't work together. It's not good for you. And it's not good for the pony."

So Anna focused on telling Acorn what she wanted him to do. She told him with her whole body, with her mind, and a tap of her heels against the pony's sides. And for the first time she really meant it.

Acorn understood Anna's message and moved forward. Anna and her pony moved as one. Riding on Acorn was great fun for Anna. And, because she would lose Acorn soon, riding him also made her sad.

When they'd covered about half of Pony Pal Trail, Anna said, "Acorn, you really are the most perfect pony. We're riding better

than we ever have. And today you're going to jump with me, too."

Anna knew that if she went to the Crandals to jump, Dr or Mrs Crandal would be sure to see her. They would want to know why she wasn't in school. There was only one place for her to go to jump with Acorn.

Anna used the reins to tell Acorn that she wanted to turn left onto the Wiggins estate. And they did. Remembering the *No Trespassing* signs and the Wiggins Witch, she thought, I won't go far. Just to the two fields with the low stone wall between them. That will be perfect for jumping.

Minutes later she was directing Acorn into the open field. She checked both sides of the low stone wall to be sure the ground was free of snow and rocks. Then she trotted Acorn a good distance away. She moved him into a canter toward the low wall. She held the reins firmly, but gave Acorn the room to go forward. She concentrated all her thoughts on going over the wall. And just like that – they flew

over it. When they landed, Acorn whinnied with delight. Anna leaned over and stroked Acorn's neck. "Good pony," she cooed.

They were getting ready for their third jump when Anna saw something moving in the woods beyond the field. In a second she saw more clearly. It was a rider in red on a black horse. The Wiggins Witch! Anna turned Acorn around. They had to get out of there.

"Hey!" the rider's voice called out.

Anna squeezed her legs against Acorn's sides. "Go," Anna ordered. They rode like the wind across the open field. Before Anna and Acorn reached the middle of the field Anna heard the pounding of hooves behind her. The sound grew louder and louder as the hooves came closer and closer.

A big black horse pulled up alongside Acorn. "Stop!" a sharp voice ordered.

It was the Wiggins Witch.

48

7

In the Wiggins Mansion

Anna had no intention of stopping. She wanted to get away from the woman in red. But Acorn, curious about the horse who'd come up alongside him, suddenly stopped. Anna pitched forward, almost over her pony's head, then fell back in the saddle. She looked up to see the Wiggins Witch turning her horse sharply around to face her and Acorn.

"I'm sorry," Anna stuttered breathlessly. "I promise I'll never come here again."

The big black horse pranced around

excitedly in front of them.

"My goodness, child," the woman was saying. "I've frightened you. I'm so sorry."

When the black horse finally stood still, Anna could see that the woman had a kind face. She didn't look at all like she'd locked herself indoors for twenty-seven years with twenty-seven cats and no toothbrush.

"I was so surprised to see a child out here," she said. "At first I thought you were one of those hunters. They've been a terrible nuisance. Then I saw it was a child and a pony and I was – well – quite surprised. Are you all right?"

Anna nodded.

The black horse, which was twice as big as Acorn, bent its head to sniff Acorn's breath. Acorn sniffed back.

"Your pony is very sweet," the woman said. "A pony is a wonderful thing to have. Do you know I still have my childhood pony? His name is Winston."

With that, Anna started to cry. The woman looked sad. "Why, what's wrong?"

she asked. "I'm sorry if I've frightened you. Is that why you're crying?"

Anna shook her head no. Now that she heard the woman's kind voice she was no longer afraid of her. What made her cry was the thought that she couldn't keep Acorn forever like the woman had kept *her* pony.

"Come," the woman directed. "Let's walk our horses around the field. The walk will do them good after our chase. We'll go side by side. If you want to tell me why you're crying, that's fine. If you don't, that's fine, too."

The smooth motion of Acorn's walk under her calmed Anna down. For the first half turn around the field they didn't speak. Finally, the woman broke the silence by saying, "Seeing you on your pony is bringing back such happy memories of my rides on Winston in these very fields. You know, you're never too old for a pony. I still go out with Winston. I harness him to a cart and drive him. When there's enough snow

I drive him with a sleigh. It's all great fun. And a pony makes a good stablemate if you get a riding horse as I did." She looked over and smiled at Anna. "By the way," she said, "my name is Wilhelmina Wiggins. But my friends call me Willie. And my horse is called Picasso."

Anna smiled back. "My name is Anna Harley," she said. "And this is Acorn. But I can't keep him the way you kept your pony."

While they took a second turn around the big field Anna told Wilhelmina Wiggins her whole sad story.

After hearing the story Ms Wiggins said, "Our horses need a rest and something to drink. You and I could use the same. Come up to the house with me and we'll take care of all of us."

At the Wiggins' stables they gave their horses water and hay. Then they led them to the paddocks. Picasso joined Winston, and Acorn was put out in an adjoining paddock. The old grey Shetland and Acorn

ran right up to the fence that separated them and whinnied friendly greetings. Picasso pranced about proudly as if to say, "I knew you two would get along."

As Anna and Ms. Wiggins walked toward the mansion, Anna asked, "Do you really live here all alone?"

"Yes, indeed," Ms. Wiggins answered. "I admit it's a lot of house for one person." She opened the front door. "Come on in."

Anna stepped into an entranceway as big as her living room at home. Facing her was a winding pink marble staircase. A painting hanging on the wall caught Anna's eye. It was the biggest, most beautiful painting she'd ever seen. Anna knew right away that the picture was a summer view of the fields where she and Ms Wiggins had just been riding. Anna also recognized the black horse and grey pony that were galloping across the painted field.

She was breathless as she stared into the painting. It looked both real and unreal at the same time. Anna knew she'd never

mistake the painting for a photograph. But she could still imagine herself walking right into the picture. Like in the most wonderful dream.

Ms Wiggins stood beside her. "You like my painting?"

Anna whispered, "It's beautiful."

"One of the reasons I keep this place is because I love drawing and painting the landscape so much."

"I like to draw," Anna said. "But you're a real artist."

Ms Wiggins laughed. "I have a feeling that you're a 'real' artist, too, Anna," she said. "While I start lunch, why don't you call your parents and tell them where you are?" She pointed to a low cabinet to her left. "There's a telephone over there."

Anna answered shyly, "They think I'm at school. I cut today."

"I see," Ms Wiggins said thoughtfully. "I guess you'd rather deal with that later then."

Anna nodded.

As she followed Ms Wiggins into the kitchen, Anna wondered how her parents would punish her for skipping school. What difference does it make? she thought. They've already given me the worst possible punishment. They are taking away Acorn.

8

More Visitors

The big kitchen windows gave Anna and Ms Wiggins a good view of the two ponies and Picasso. Anna was glad to be eating Ms Wiggins's delicious soup in the warm kitchen. And she liked talking to Ms Wiggins.

Ms Wiggins told Anna that she hadn't been a good student, either. "I had an impossible time with spelling," Ms. Wiggins said. "Even now I make spelling mistakes."

"Same with me," Anna said.

Then Ms Wiggins asked Anna a lot of

questions about how she learned and how she solved problems. Ms Wiggins listened thoughtfully to Anna's answers. "Anna, I think that you are dyslexic, just like me," she said. "That means you're very bright, but you reverse or rearrange letters."

"How come you know all this stuff and my teachers don't?" Anna asked.

"You're probably so clever that you've fooled them into thinking you can read better than you do," Ms Wiggins answered.

"I haven't fooled Mr Livingston," Anna said. "The work in Year Five is a lot harder than the other grades."

"A good tutor would be a great help to you," Ms Wiggins said. "Though I don't see how taking your pony away will help."

"That's just going to make me sad," Anna said.

After biscuits and milk for dessert, Ms Wiggins led Anna up two flights of the winding marble staircase, down a hall, and into a large room with windows on the ceiling.

Anna loved the room immediately.

"This is my art studio," Ms Wiggins said. Anna slowly walked around the studio. There was so much that interested her she didn't know where to go first. At one end of the room there were two easels with large unfinished landscape paintings. On a wooden table she saw neat rows of oil paint tubes and a bunch of paintbrushes of all sizes standing like bouquets in old jars. Paintings and drawings of the Wiggins estate were everywhere.

Anna thought that Ms Wiggins was the luckiest person. She could paint and draw whenever she wanted. She had two beautiful horses and probably never had to remember the multiplication tables.

"If I'm not up here," Ms Wiggins told Anna, "I'm usually outside with the animals."

"That's what I want to do when I grow up," Anna said. "Paint and have horses."

"I hope you can," Ms Wiggins told her. "But for now I wish you could get your

60

teachers and parents to understand your difficulty with schoolwork. Have you ever talked to them the way you talked to me? You know, explaining how you learn and what your problems are?"

"I only told Acorn," Anna said.

"I think you should try hard to explain the situation to your parents and your teachers," Ms Wiggins said.

Ms Wiggins walked towards the window and looked out. "My goodness!" she exclaimed. "More children on ponies are coming this way. It's turning out to be a very social day."

Anna ran to her side. Through the window she saw her Pony Pals galloping towards Wiggins mansion.

"I'd bet you know those girls," Ms Wiggins said.

"We're all best friends," Anna told her. "They must be looking for me."

Ms Wiggins smiled. "Well," she said, "I suppose we should invite them in.

As they ran down the curving staircase,

Anna thought how smart and brave her friends were to trail her to the Wiggins mansion. And how frightened they must be of Ms Wiggins. So when Ms Wiggins opened the door, Anna blurted out, "It's OK. She's nice.

Pam and Lulu knew what Anna said was true because Ms Wiggins had a warm and friendly smile.

Soon there were two more ponies in the paddocks outside the kitchen window. And two more girls around the kitchen table eating buscuits and drinking milk.

Pam and Lulu explained what happened after school. They went to Anna's house to see how she was feeling and there was no one there. Then they went out back and saw that Acorn wasn't in the paddock.

"We were afraid he'd already gone back to Mr Olson's," Pam said. "Then we saw all the hoofprints and footprints in the patches of snow leading to the trail; we knew you'd gone out with Acorn."

"Did you tell my parents?" Anna asked fearfully.

"Oh, no," Lulu exclaimed. "We thought you ran away. We wanted to find you and bring you back before they found out. We tracked you by following Acorn's hoofprints.

Pam grinned at Anna. "Acorn finally jumped with you didn't he?"

"Yup," Anna beamed. "Twice."

"We worked that out, too," Lulu told her. "But we were really scared when we saw there were two different sets of hoofprints."

"Did you think some mean, bad person had kidnapped her?" Ms Wiggins asked.

The three girls sheepishly smiled at one another. "Sort of," Lulu admitted.

After Anna and Ms Wiggins congratulated Pam and Lulu on their detective work, Ms Wiggins wanted to know all about the girls and their families. Each girl told her where she lived and where her parents worked.

Ms Wiggins said that she knew Pam's father because he was her veterinarian. She

also knew Anna's mother because they had gone to Wiggins Primary together. "And I drop by her café once in awhile," she told Anna, "for a little chat and one of her chocolate brownies."

But of all the parents, Ms Wiggins was most interested in Lulu's father. "He travels all over the world studying wildlife and writes about it," Lulu explained. "Sometimes I go with him. But not this time. He's in the Amazon jungle and I'd miss too much school. That's why I'm staying with my grandmother this year. She has a beauty shop on Main Street."

"When I wore my hair short, I used to visit your grandmother's salon more often," Ms Wiggins said.

"I like your hair just the way it is now," Anna told her.

The other girls agreed that Ms Wiggins's long black hair looked nice.

Before they left, Ms Wiggins told Pam and Lulu that she thought that Anna was dyslexic and explained what that meant. "I

bet you three girls can work together to help her keep Acorn." Ms Wiggins smiled.

"We'll try our best," Lulu said.

"We've solved lots of problems together," Pam added.

When the Pony Pals were back on their own trail it was time for Anna and Lulu to say goodbye to Pam.

"Ms Wiggins gave us an important clue about why you have trouble with schoolwork," Pam said. "Now it's up to us to do something about it. Tomorrow morning let's meet before school starts and come up with a plan."

"Each of us should write out an idea of how Anna can keep Acorn," Lulu added.

The Pony Pals decided to meet the next day at 8:15 when the school building opened for early students.

But that afternoon, as Anna rode Acorn home along the trail, she wondered if her problems weren't too big for the Pony Pals.

9

Three Ideas Too Late

The next morning at 8:15 the caretaker opened the doors to Wiggins Primary. The Pony Pals went in and walked down the hall together.

"Did you get into trouble for skipping school?" Pam asked Anna.

"Yeah," she answered. "My mum found out when she called Mr Livingston to make an appointment to talk about me." Anna remembered the sad look on her mother's face. "And my dad said I did it because of Acorn. He said that it

just proves I shouldn't have a pony."

"Don't worry," Pam told her. "We're going to help you."

The girls put their coats in their lockers, sat down on the floor, and took out their notebooks.

"OK," Lulu said. "Who's going first? How about you, Pam?"

Pam read.

> Tell Mr Livingston that we think Anna is dyslexic and that he should give her a special test. Also, get him to tell Anna's parents all about dyslexia.

"That's perfect," Lulu said. "And all three of us should talk to him, not just Anna."

"Here's my idea," Anna said. "It's connected to Pam's."

SPECSHEL TUDOR 4 ME

"I don't know how to spell 'special tutor,'" Anna said.

"But look how well you draw," Pam exclaimed. "I couldn't do that. That's what Ms Wiggins meant by, 'Different brains work in different ways.'"

"Just the same," Anna said, "I want to be able to read and spell better. And getting extra homework isn't enough help. Ms Wiggins said I need a tutor. I wouldn't mind studying a lot if I could keep Acorn."

"That's where my idea comes in," Lulu said. She read from her notebook:

> I will do Anna's pony chores so she has more time to study. It's only fair because I've been boarding Snow White at the Harley's for free.

68

Anna smiled at Lulu. "Thanks," she said, "but only if I really don't have time to do the chores myself."

"That's a great idea, Lulu," Pam said.

Anna agreed. "My parents are always saying that doing Acorn's chores takes up too much of my time. But if Lulu's doing the work, they can't use that as an excuse for taking him away from me."

The Pony Pals decided to put Pam's plan into action first. They rushed off to their classroom to talk to Mr Livingston before the school day began.

The three girls told Mr Livingston that they thought Anna was dyslexic. He said that he thought the same thing when he analyzed Anna's scores on the standardized reading tests. "That's why I've asked your parents to meet me," he told Anna. "I need their permission to have you tested. If you're dyslexic, we'll have no trouble getting a specialist to work with you a couple of afternoons a week after school."

He leaned forward over his desk and spoke in his most serious teacher voice. "But, Anna, you're going to have to put in some hard work."

"I will," Anna said, "I promise. I want to do better in school. But I want to be able to keep my pony, too."

Mr Livingston said that all he could do was explain what dyslexia was to Anna's parents and arrange for extra help.

"Can't you tell them that it's not her fault that she's not getting good grades?" Pam pleaded.

"Absolutely," he said. He looked down at his appointment book. "I'm seeing them Friday morning before school."

The warning bell rang signalling that kids in the hall should go to their home rooms. Now the other kids would be coming into the room.

"Mr Livingston," Lulu said, "Friday is two days away. You've got to talk to Anna's parents before then. Or Anna might lose Acorn. Please, please, please."

70

"Couldn't you call them up or something?" Pam asked.

"The sooner the better," Anna added.

Now there were twenty other kids in the room. They were talking to one another and yelling good morning to Mr Livingston.

"I'll see what I can do," Mr Livingston said. "Now go to your places."

Before the Pony Pals separated to go to their seats, they exchanged smiles. Their first idea had worked out really well.

After school that day the Pony Pals headed over to Anna's house. Their next step was to tell Mrs Harley all about what Ms Wiggins and what Mr Livingston said about dyslexia.

As they ran down Main Street toward Anna's house, Pam said, "Lulu, don't forget to tell Anna's mother how you'll do a lot of the chores for Acorn."

They ran up the outside stairs to the back door. Pam got there first. "Anna," she said, "the door's locked. Is this one of the

afternoons your mum works at the café?"

Anna couldn't answer. She was standing on the landing staring out at the pony paddock. For a few seconds she didn't say anything.

When she finally spoke it was in a low whisper. "Acorn's gone."

Pam and Lulu could see in a glance that Snow White was alone in the backyard paddock.

Anna had tears running down her cheeks. "They didn't even let me say goodbye."

10

Where's Acorn?

The Pony Pals went out to the paddock to be absolutely, positively sure that Acorn wasn't there.

As they climbed through the fence rails into the small field, Lulu said, "Maybe he squeezed in behind the shelter. Some animals can make themselves very small."

"But not ponies," Pam commented. Snow White galloped over to them and whinnied. Anna thought she sounded upset. "Maybe Acorn's hurt," she told her friends.

The Pony Pals looked around the bushes

and trees along the inside edges of the paddock. And they checked behind the shelter. Snow White followed them everywhere. But there was only one pony in Acorn's paddock. And it wasn't Acorn. They all knew he'd been given back.

Snow White whinnied again.

"She's telling us she misses Acorn," Anna said quietly.

Pam and Lulu each put an arm around Anna's shoulders. Pam told her, "When we tell your parents about the dyslexia thing maybe they'll let you buy Acorn after all."

"Let's go to the café and see if your mum's there. OK?" Lulu said.

Anna nodded. She was feeling so sad she couldn't talk. Even to her best friends.

"Don't give up hope, Anna," Lulu said. "We'll get him back."

Through the front window of Off-Main Café, Anna saw her mother walking to the back booth with two cups of coffee. "She's there," she told the others. "Now she's sitting down with whoever's in that booth."

Pam cautioned, "OK, guys, no matter what happens, we must stay calm. It's hard enough to explain this dyslexia stuff. Everybody agree?"

Lulu and Pam looked at Anna. Anna nodded. "I promise I won't cry." She paused before adding, "Unless I think it'll help."

The three Pony Pals were about to walk into the café, when Pam motioned them to duck and said, "Quick, hide."

"I don't think she saw us," Pam whispered as they huddled down under the café window.

"Who?" Lulu and Anna asked.

"Ms Wiggins," Pam said. "That's who. She's the one in the booth."

"So why didn't we go in?" Lulu asked. "She's nice. She's on our side."

"That's exactly why," Pam advised "Maybe she came to talk to your mother about you, Anna. We have to give her plenty of time to explain about dyslexia."

The girls took turns sneaking looks in

through the café window.

During Pam's turn they learned that Anna's mother got a telephone call.

During Anna's turn they learned that Ms Wiggins and Anna's mother went to the counter to get brownies. And now they were sitting at the counter.

During her turn Lulu said, "They're laughing."

"It's time to make our move," Pam said.

The Pony Pals walked into the café. Anna's mother saw them first. "Well," she said with a laugh, "look what the cat dragged in."

Ms Wiggins smiled at the girls, too. She said, "Anna, I've been telling your mother—"

But she didn't finish the sentence because Anna wailed, "Mummy, how could you send Acorn away? I didn't even get to say goodbye. . ."

The cook looked out from the kitchen to find out what was going on.

The only sound in the café was Anna's

78

tearful voice asking, "Don't you know how much I love him?"

"It was Mr Olson's idea to come after Acorn today," Anna's mother said. "Your father and I thought it might be easier on you. I left you a note in the kitchen explaining everything."

"We didn't go into the house," Pam told Mrs Harley. Then she added quickly, "Mr Livingston thinks Anna is dyslexic. Ms Wiggins does, too."

"That's what Willie and I've been talking about," Anna's mother told the girls.

Lulu jumped in with her idea. "If you buy Acorn for Anna, I promise to do her afternoon chores in the paddock. That way she'll have lots of time to study. It'll be my way of paying for Snow White to stay there. I don't mind at all. It's only fair."

"Mr Livingston said Anna can have a special tutor after school. For free," Pam added.

Anna listened to all of this and thought, I have wonderful friends. Now if I could

only get my pony back. . .

She walked over to her mother. "I'm sorry I yelled," she said. "And I'm sorry I'm stupid."

Pam, Lulu, Ms Wiggins, and Anna's mother shouted in unison, "You're not stupid!"

They all laughed. All except Anna. She had only one thing on her mind. And it wasn't a laughing matter. That's why she was still crying.

"Maybe you'd like to hear what your father and I were just talking about on the phone. Do you think you could stop crying and listen?"

Anna nodded and looked up at her mother.

"Mr Livingston called your father at the shop a little while ago. He basically said the same thing Willie just told me. About this dyslexia business. Mr Livingston also feels that taking away Acorn is too much like a punishment for something that hasn't been your fault.

So we've decided to buy Acorn for—"

The Pony Pals didn't hear the rest of the sentence because they were jumping up and down with shouts and squeals and giving each other high fives.

Then they stopped suddenly. They'd all had the same thought at the same time.

Lulu was the first to put it into words. "Mr Olson said he has someone else who wanted Acorn."

"That must be why he took him back right away," Pam said.

"Oh, no," Anna said. "Those other people could be picking up Acorn right now!"

11

A Ride with Winston

Two truck drivers walked into Off-Main Café.

Mrs Harley told Ms Wiggins and the girls, "I've got to get back to work." She got off the stool and went up to meet the men.

Anna followed Mrs Harley as she led the customers to a booth. She was pleading with her mother, "But, Mum, you've got to sign the papers and give me a cheque. I have to get to Olson's before somebody else takes Acorn. We've got to hurry."

"We're in a bit of a hurry ourselves,

ma'am," one of the customers told Mrs Harley.

Pam came over to the booth. 'I'll take their order, Mrs Harley," Pam said. Then she told the men, "Our specials today are lasagna or meatloaf with mashed potatoes."

Lulu came to the booth and handed out menus. "I'll be right back with water and rolls," she said.

Mrs Harley was smiling as she handed Pam her pad and pencil. "Pam will take your order," she said to her customers.

Two more customers were walking through the front door. Lulu ran up to greet them and to ask them where they'd like to sit.

As Anna followed her mother back to the counter she slipped off her backpack and unzipped it. "I have the sale papers right here," she told her mother. She pulled out the page that Mr Olsen had given her and put it on the counter. "Just sign it and write a cheque. OK?"

83

Ms Wiggins handed Mrs Harley a pen. As her mother carefully read the page Anna remembered her nightmare. What if Mr Olson already sold Acorn to someone else?

Finally her mother signed the document and wrote a cheque. "Now," she said, "I'd better get back to work. How will you get over to Olson's farm?"

"I can drive her," Ms Wiggins offered.

"Do you know where it is?" Anna asked.

"I do," Ms Wiggins answered.

Mrs Harley went back to her customers and Pam and Lulu followed Ms Wiggins and Anna. When they were outside, Ms Wiggins turned to them and said, "I'm afraid I only have room for Anna." She smiled at Anna, "I'm glad you're small."

The Pony Pals exchanged questioning glances. How could Ms Wiggins have a car so small that Anna's size would make a difference? Pam and Lulu were so curious about this situation that they walked around to the parking lot with Anna.

A pony's neigh greeted them. There, in the fenced-in area behind the parking lot, the Pony Pals saw Ms Wiggins's pony, Winston. The pony cart stood in a parking space near two big trucks.

"Don't worry," Ms Wiggins told Anna as she hitched Winston to the cart. "He'll get you there in a hurry. Winston can put on the steam when I ask him to. Besides, I know an old trail that's a shortcut to Olson's."

Anna enjoyed the pony cart ride so much that for a few minutes she forgot that they might be too late to get her own pony back. And when Ms Wiggins let her take the reins on an easy part of the trail, Anna imagined herself years from now with Acorn pulling her in a cart.

When they got to Olson's, Ms Wiggins drove Winston right past the parking area and over the field toward the barn. She told Anna, "This is one of the great advantages of a pony and cart. You don't always need a road."

But Anna wasn't paying much attention to what Ms Wiggins was saying. She was checking out the paddocks to see if Acorn was among Olson's dozen or so horses and ponies.

"He's not here," she told Ms Wiggins.

"Well, maybe he's in the barn," Ms Wiggins said. "Look, there's Reggie Olson."

Anna saw he was standing in front of the barn. He waved at them and called out, "Hey, hey, Willie. You ready to sell me that old pony?"

When they reached Mr Olson, Ms Wiggins told Winston, "Whoa." She smiled at Mr Olson. "Reggie, you know I'll never sell Winston. I've brought my young friend over to buy her pony."

Mr Olson slapped his thigh happily and exclaimed, "The Harley girl! I knew you'd be wanting something bigger than that" Shetland. And lucky for you, young lady, that I still have the Morgan."

Anna jumped out of the cart. "I don't want another horse. I want Acorn back."

86

She looked around desperately. "Where is he?"

"I have another family that wants to buy him," Mr Olson said.

Anna held up the paper and said, "My mother signed it." She held up the cheque. "And here's the money. I have to have Acorn," she said with determination. "He can't go to someone else."

"Reggie, Anna and Acorn are quite a pair," Ms Wiggins said. "You can find another pony for your customer."

Mr Olson took the document and cheque from Anna. She held her breath while he studied them.

"Well," Mr Olson said slowly, "the other people haven't signed anything. To be perfectly honest, they haven't even seen Acorn yet."

He nodded over his shoulder toward the barn. "He's in there," Mr Olson said.

"Thank you. Oh, thank you so much," Anna said. Then she ran into the barn. She passed several stalls of horses and ponies

before she found her pony. "Acorn, Acorn," she called out happily.

Acorn was so glad to see her that he stopped eating. Anna opened the stall door and went in to give him a hug.

Mr Olson came up to the stall. "I can't trailer him back to your place until tomorrow," he said.

"I'll ride him back," Anna told him. "And I want the same saddle and everything."

A few minutes later Acorn was saddled up. Anna led him out of the barn and over to where Ms Wiggins and Winston were waiting for her. "You lead the way back, Anna," Ms Wiggins said as she climbed into the seat of her driving cart.

Anna mounted Acorn, found her stirrups, and took proper hold of the reins. Then she pressed her legs against her pony's sides. "Let's go Acorn," she said.

Acorn didn't move.

Anna remembered what Mrs Crandal had taught her. She had to concentrate and

88

tell Acorn what she wanted. She focused very hard and used her whole body and mind to tell Acorn what to do. And they moved forward.

As she trotted along the old trail on her pony Anna thought, I guess you and I are a lot alike, Acorn. To get along we've had to do things our own way. Now it's time for both of us to make some changes. You're already learning how to work with me. And I'm going to have to work with my tutor.

A minute later Anna laughed out loud. Acorn was hers for keeps. And now she knew that no matter how big she got, with a pony cart she could ride him forever. Just like Ms Wiggins and Winston behind her.

Anna took a deep breath of the crisp winter air and looked between Acorn's ears at the path ahead. She couldn't wait to show this new trail to her Pony Pals.

Dear Reader:

I am having a lot of fun researching and writing books about the Pony Pals. I've met many interesting kids and adults who love ponies. And I've visited some wonderful ponies at homes, farms, and riding schools.

Before writing Pony Pals I wrote fourteen novels for children and young adults. Four of these were honoured by Children's Choice Awards.

I live in Sharon, Connecticut, with my husband, Lee, and our dog, Willie. Our daughter is all grown up and has her own apartment in New York City.

Besides writing novels I like to draw, paint, garden, and swim. I didn't have a pony when I was growing up, but I have always loved them and dreamt about riding. Now I take riding lessons on a horse named Saz.

I like reading and writing about ponies as much as I do riding. Which proves to me that you don't have to ride a pony to love them. And you certainly don't need a pony to be a Pony Pal.

Happy Reading,

Jeanne Betancourt